Stranded

A Shell Harbor Mermaid Romance
Book One

Lauren Smith

ISBN: 978-1-962760-63-8 (e-book edition)

ISBN: 978-1-962760-64-5 (print edition)

ONE

Hudson Clark didn't believe in mermaids. Surely no one in the twenty-first century could... but if he did, he would have to face the fact that mermaids had killed his parents. But mermaids were a myth. The dark, turbulent waters of the Atlantic always made people see things that weren't there, like shapes just beneath the water that looked too much like things that weren't real.

He peered into the black waters while he guided his yacht through the churning seas, attempting to get back to land. He was seeing things that shouldn't be there. Unable to shake the feeling that something watched him from the obsidian waves. The hairs on the back of his neck stood on end, warning him that he wasn't alone. The chill in the air and the darkening evening skies seemed heavy with a danger of another kind. Hudson regretting going out so late in the day, not when he'd had a sailor's sense the wind would shift and the skies would darken.

It was easy to get turned around and become lost in the North Atlantic when one lost sight of the shore during storms, especially at night. His eyes had started to play tricks on him in the last half hour. One minute he'd see a flash of silver upon the water or hear a piercing wail from beyond the glow of his boat's electric lights. A few times he could swear he heard his name echo across the water. But the sea played tricks upon men, and had been doing so since mankind first looked out across the endless blue ocean and asked themselves: *What if...*

His yacht hit a wave hard, and the impact jarred through him, making his very bones ache where he stood on the bridge.

"Hudson..." His name came as a whisper despite the wind howling across the deck.

His uncle had warned him never to sail in the dark, not after the storm and wreck that had taken his parents and nearly claimed his uncle's life.

They're out there, Hudson. Waiting, watching. If they call your name, It's already too late.

He could still see his Uncle Jason's dark-brown eyes glinting with a hint of madness as he whispered those words, lying in a hospital suffering from dehydration and exhaustion. Jason had been on the sailboat with Hudson's parents the day a nor'easter struck the coast. The sailboat had been pushed too fast toward shore by the storm and struck a rocky area where it sank.

Jason had been unable to get the cabin door open to save Hudson parents, barely managing to escape himself. He'd floated on a piece of wreckage for two days before the Coast Guard found him. By then he was suffering from delusions and screaming about mermaids. That had been seven years ago, but it felt like a lifetime to Hudson. He was twenty-nine now, and losing his parents at twenty-two, just when he'd gotten out of college and was supposed to have a bright future ahead of him, had aged him and changed the trajectory of his life. He'd given up the investment banking job he'd been offered by one of Manhattan's top firms and instead took his inheritance from his parents and returned home to Shell Harbor be near his uncle and the sea which had taken so much from him already.

Jason refused to go anywhere near the ocean now. He'd left his job catching lobsters and bought a restaurant in town to run during the tourist season. Jason never went to the beach anymore and certainly didn't get on anymore boats. When storms blew in, he hunkered down at his restaurant or at his home, practically barricading himself against the raging winds as if he could escape his past.

Hudson on the other hand, hadn't avoided the water. Something about it filled him with a blinding rage, yet it drew him in, whispering briny apologies upon a gentle breeze. To make a living, he gave coastal tours on the yacht he bought with some of his trust-fund money. It kept him out on the water, every day going back to the place where his parents had died. And while that rubbed some salt in his wounds, it also kept his parents present in his memory.

The wind changed and he held onto the helm, holding his boat, the *Splash*, as steady as he could. Something hit the boat hard, in a repeated thudding, too quick and too steady to be waves.

His training perked up his senses and his sailor's experience provided him with an answer and in a breath he was cursing as he realized he might have hit rocks. A blast of rain lashed the decks, blinding as the water reflected off his boat lights. He strained his eyes through the sheets of moisture outside of the cabin, looking for the lighthouse lantern that he'd been charting towards, but the conditions had obscured it completed now.

Suddenly the lights on his ship flickered, the moment's quiet as the buzz of electricity halted serving only to heighten the sound of a wail as it rippled across the dark waters beyond the bridge.

Thud!

Before he could interrogate himself over what the wail

could have come from, a black mass swept over the decks and deposited something hard on the bow ahead of him.

He cursed as a sudden blast of rain lashed the deck in blinding sheets. He couldn't even see the lighthouse anymore through the windows on the bridge. The lights on his vessel flickered suddenly and a lone wail rippled across the dark waters just beyond the bow.

Thud! A black mass swept over the deck with the next wave, and something landed on the bow ahead of him. When the water receded and the boat righted itself, he glimpsed the shape again. It was still there on the deck. Had a large sturgeon landed on the boat? It wasn't entirely impossible. They did prefer the cold water, and right now the Atlantic was like ice given it was late September.

Whatever it was, he couldn't put it back in the water until he found his way back to shore. Whatever it was could wait. Another wave had him regripping the wheel and pushing against the swell that was tipping his yacht to the right, forcing him to face the fact that he had more important matters to attend to, like not getting capsized. Hudson turned the wheel of the ship, fighting for his life and the life of his vessel. Suddenly the wind and rain railing against the yacht began to ease off. And through the thinning storm, he saw a flash...was that a light? He squinted through the rain.

Yes, it was a light! It appeared on the horizon through the lessening rain. It was the lighthouse. The harbor was less than a mile away. Tension bled out of his stiff shoulders, and he let out a breath he hadn't realized he'd been holding. He steered the helm a little to the port side and aimed directly for the shining beacon of light. The rain and wind began to fade and it wasn't long before he found his way back to the harbor. Now that the seas had settled, he felt like he could risk leaving the helm to go push the fish back overboard. He killed the engine, knowing the boat would drift a little but he could correct it soon enough. The waves here were soft and normal, nothing like the swells far back out to sea.

He grabbed a flashlight from where it was strapped to the wall by the yacht's controls. Then he left the bridge and walked toward the bow. He shined a light ahead of him to illuminate his path. Seaweed was scattered on the deck and formed a large pile. Had that been what he'd seen? Just seaweed?

No, he glimpsed a soft slash of something pale in the middle of the blackish-green mess of the watery plants. It was a face. A *human* face.

"Oh God," he gasped. A body had washed up on his yacht. He ran toward it, praying he had a chance to save the person, but knowing the odds were slim to none. He hadn't seen any other boats nearby, so it was unfortunately likely that the body had been floating in the water a while. The horrifying sorrow that knowledge invoked made his stomach churn. Whoever it was ... had drowned just like his parents had. Hudson fought off a violent shudder and forced himself to focus.

He crouched and began peeling away the lanky bits of seaweed to expose a woman's face. Her features were delicate, beautiful, and lacked the swollen appearance of a body that had been in water for a long time. She looked young, so damned young it broke his heart. She couldn't have been more than eighteen or nineteen, if he had to guess. He removed more of the seaweed and cursed at discovering her upper body was bare. She was *naked*.

What the hell had happened that she'd ended up in the ocean without clothes? Cuts marred her pale luminescent skin. He took note of each wound—one along her cheek, another over her breastbone, and a bleeding gash several inches long across her ribs. She was still bleeding ... But dead bodies didn't bleed. That meant she was alive.

He hastily dragged more seaweed off her so could see the rest of her injuries. But his fingers froze as they encountered the slick, silky feel of something foreign where her hip bone should have been. He moved the flashlight down her body to her lower half. His fingers rested not on skin ... but scales. They were a greenish-blue color that seemed to shimmer and change in the light. Fish scales ... beginning at the girl's waist.

What the fuck?

He scraped more seaweed away and stared at the large pale green-blue tail that stretched along the deck where the girl's legs should have been. A dull roar started in his ears as he stared at the girl—er, fish—on his boat.

They're out there, Hudson ... mermaids. They'll drown you. Again his uncle's words floated across his mind. No, mermaids couldn't be real. They couldn't...but the seamless line of human skin turning to dark green-blue scales argued that this girl wasn't human.

In that moment he knew two things. First ... there was a mermaid on his yacht, and second ... Uncle Jason was not crazy.

The woman ... uh ... mermaid, made a soft sound and suddenly moved, turning her face toward him. Hudson leapt back, even though the creature's movement was slow and sluggish. All he could hear was his uncle's warnings about how they'd drown him.

"Hud—son..." His name escaped her lips in a broken breath and Hudson's heart jolted in his chest. This creature knew his name. Her eyes opened and he saw the aquamarine irises glowing unnaturally in the reflection of the flashlight he aimed at her face. Her eyes were beautiful ... So beautiful it hurt to look at her.

"Hurt..." She breathed out in pain and one of her slender hands hovered over the gash above her lower ribs as though afraid to touch it. Her gaze held his and everything around him fell away into the black water. There was only her ... and the fact that she was hurt.

He set the slender flashlight between his teeth the way a pirate would hold a cutlass and bent down, one arm sliding beneath her back and the other beneath the middle of her tail. Hudson he lifted her up. She wasn't heavy, but rather the perfect weight in his arms. She made a soft little sound of pain but curled her arms around his neck. The scent of the sea, clean with a hint of brine clung to her skin. He carried her through the narrow passage toward the bridge and then up a flight of steps to the doors that led to the upper deck where he stayed in the master cabin. The master cabin featured a large, carpeted master bedroom, and a lavish bathroom. Hudson carefully set her down on the floor in front of the bed. She was breathing slowly and shallowly, and he knew she'd likely lost a decent amount of blood in the water before she'd ended up on his boat.

"Stay there," he ordered, hoping that she couldn't go anywhere because he didn't want her getting hurt further.

She didn't move as he fetched the first aid kit from the bathroom. When he returned, he knelt beside her and opened the red plastic lid and dug around for antiseptic and a needle and thread. He had done this once before when a tourist had slipped and cut his arm while drinking on one of his tours. But the position of this cut was more intimate—just below her breasts. Hudson's hands were steady as he rubbed a cloth over the wound and then prepared the needle and the suture thread. The shock of stitching up a wound on a mermaid would register later, he was certain, but for now he was glad to be focused.

"This going to hurt like hell," he warned.

The mermaid's hands curled into fists in the plush carpet, and she shut her eyes. He stitched as quickly as he could while still being careful not to make any mistakes. His brave little mermaid made not a single sound, but if she had, he would have stopped at once and wrapped his arms around her. Something about her just demanded be protect her, care for her. He'd always been protective and caring for the girls he dated, but this...creature drew so much more of that instinct out of him.

"Done," he breathed as he tied knots in the thread.

The creature let out a breath, her breasts rising and then falling as she relaxed into another deeper breath. He was suddenly very aware again that she was naked ... or half naked. He'd seen plenty of naked women in his day. But this was different ... this was strange. This woman— *creature*—was affecting him more than she should. She wasn't even human.

Yet he couldn't tear his eyes off her face or her body. Her dark-green-blue tail that shimmered with droplets of seawater called to him. He was touching her before he could even think about what he was doing. He stroked the scales at her hip, feeling their smoothness beneath his palm. Her bright-blue eyes traced the movement as he stroked her, but she didn't move. Was she scared of him?

"I won't hurt you," he promised, and his eyes roved up her body to focus on her face again. She looked so god damn innocent and sweet as she nibbled on her bottom lip and her big blue eyes stared at him. Was that what made her so dangerous? Was she truly a ruthless killer like his uncle believed?

"You said my name," he spoke softly, his palm still gliding over her tail as he studied her with fascination.

"Hudson," she said, her voice soft, slightly husky, and incredibly musical.

"Do you speak English?" he asked and finally pulled his hand away from her tail.

"Yes." She sat up a little, her full breasts pressing together when she curled one arm protectively around her body, as if she were shy. Could mermaids be shy? A distant part of him wondered if he'd fallen during the storm and hit his head and now was dreaming about mermaids. Beautiful, wide-eyed mermaids that were making him hunger for things ... *mad* things ... like wanting to kiss one just to see if he would be drowned in passion.

He gave himself a mental shake and the fog of confusing desire cleared.

"You're a mermaid," he said bluntly. Despite her apparent exhaustion, she gave him an *Are you serious?* look.

"You're real," he said, feeling more like an idiot than ever, but dammit, he had just learned a mythological creature existed and it was on his boat right in front of him.

"Can I stay here?" the mermaid asked, her face still pale. Was she supposed to be pale? He didn't know anything about mermaids.

"You want to stay on my boat? Why?" That was something he hadn't expected her to ask.

"I got separated from my pod and was attacked by sharks. If that wave hadn't washed me on your deck..." She didn't finish but her body began to shudder like she was going into shock. Hudson had the sudden crazy urge to wrap his arms around her and tuck her against his body, holding her until the trembling passed. But he didn't. That would only lead to trouble.

"Your pod?"

"My family ... the other merpeople I live with."

That created a thousand more questions, but Hudson knew now was not the time to ask them. She was exhausted and injured.

"I guess you can, but I have to get into the harbor and dock my ship. I can't stay out at sea in case the storm moves inland."

She nodded. "That's okay. I'll only be here as long as I have to." She glanced around his bedroom.

"Do you need to be in the water to rest?" He thought

of the large Jacuzzi tub in the bathroom. He could put her in there for a little bit.

She seemed to think it over before she nodded. "It would make me more comfortable and help me heal faster, but I don't have to be in water."

"Then that's what we'll do. Hold onto me," he urged as he reached for her again, cradling her in his arms. She fit so perfectly there, but he tried not to think about how good it felt to have her in his hold. Her tail draped down over his arm, the fins tickling the side of his left knee. She wrapped her arms around his neck, pressing her cheek against his shoulder. She was cold to the touch, and he didn't know if that was a natural or if he should be worried.

Hudson carried her into the bathroom and set her down on the edge of the large tub. Then he began running water. Her blue-green tail stretched down into the tub, her tailfin wriggled a little at the touch of the cold water that first splashed into the tub as he plugged the bottom. He tested the temperature, making it warmer than she was probably used to. Her skin had goosebumps and she was still shivering, and he didn't think that could be natural.

"Do you need me to add salt or something?" God he really did sound insane. Maybe he was going crazy.

"No, it's fine." She eased herself down into the water that was pooling at the bottom of the tub and curled up, her tail bent like she'd folded her legs in a fetal position.

Her fins rippled in a slow pattern as she seemed to absorb the hot water in relief. Then she closed her eyes and let out a soft sigh that reached his ears despite the sound of the splashing water in the large tub. Her fingers moved gently in the water, as if it soothed her.

"I'll be just outside this room if you need me. And please...don't try to leave alright? I want to make sure those stitches help you heal and I'll need to remove them before you head back into the sea." He couldn't believe he was having this conversation with a mermaid but she let out a soft sigh, that sounded almost...content? Could an injured mermaid in a hot bath be content? God, he didn't know, but he hoped she was. A contented creature would be less likely to flee in the middle of the night, and he had so many questions he wanted to ask her. But first, he needed to sleep, he was damned exhausted.

Hudson stood there a long moment, watching the water creep up over her body until her hair moved with the currents and her face was completely covered. It was wild, to stare at the mermaid underwater in his tub and know she wasn't drowning, that she could stay submerged beneath the surface and just breathe. Did she have gills hidden somewhere? He wanted to know but she looked so peaceful now he didn't want to bother her. That left him alone with his own thoughts.

Mermaids were real. What the hell was he supposed to do now that he knew the truth? Did this mean other supernatural or mythical creatures were real? Were vampires, werewolves, and unicorns real? His entire world had just been flipped upside down and fuck if he knew what to do about it.

When the tub was full and the mermaid was fully submerged under the water, apparently asleep, Hudson turned the faucet off. Then he closed the bathroom door. He retrieved his cell phone from the bridge and tucked it into the pocket of his shorts before he took control of the yacht. They had drifted back out to sea while he'd been busy below deck with her, so he started the engines up again and steered toward the lighthouse and the small town of Shell Harbor and into his berth at the docks. It had been about half an hour since he'd escaped the storm, and it was almost midnight. He had to tell his uncle but it could wait until he'd had more time to speak to the girl. Jason had to know what he had found. The question was, what would he do about it? All he knew at that moment was mermaids were real.

Talia rested for a long while, half asleep in the deliciously warm water. After a long while had passed, her eyes opened and she looked up to the surface of the now-still water to see the ceiling of the bathroom above her. It had been two years since she'd been become this creature. She'd been born human, and had been drowning when a pod of mermaids found her and gave her a choice: accept the change into one of them, or drown. She had chosen the change.

And now she was bound to the sea. She could regain her legs when the moon rose at night. It was her one special gift from the sea. Others in her pod had different gifts, but the moon's power was hers and hers alone. She lifted her head and stared at the moonlight coming through the window. How long had it been since she'd let herself become human? At least five or six months. The change was a little painful, but what hurt more was knowing she would have to go back to the water, back to her life in the dark depths of the sea. Because of that, she'd avoided the change—so she could avoid the regret of losing her humanity again and again.

The water began to heal her bit by bit and after an hour she used her fingernails to cut the stitches on her ribs and pull the thread loose. Her skin was red, but that soon would fade. Tonight she'd had a close call. It was always dangerous to be far away from the pod, but when the storms raged and the blue water turned dark, she felt the land calling to her. Whenever she could, she slipped away from the others and swam toward shore.

Usually she would wander the coastline, searching for

something she could never seem to find. Only tonight ... she had found Hudson. Her older mer sister Isabel had spoken of a pair of humans who perished at sea seven years ago. Isabel had seen them trying to escape a cabin as it flooded with water, but couldn't get out. She'd swum to the cabin windows and heard them talking through the water as they'd struggled for their final breaths. Their last words had been of their son that they would never see again. *Hudson.* They had been offered the change just like her, but they had refused. They clung to each other as the water rose and they perished in each other's arms. The mermaids had watched with sorrow. A third human with them had survived the wreck. He had seen Isabel's pod circling him, watching him, trying to help him if he started to drown, but he'd survived by floating on debris and was rescued by humans.

Talia had come to the pod years later, but she knew all about Hudson because he traveled the coast on his ship the *Splash*, and the pod watched over him from a distance. They felt it was their solemn duty after not being able to save his parents.

Hudson. Beautiful Hudson. She found herself smiling. She'd never been close enough to see him clearly before. He'd always been a distant masculine figure on the deck of his yacht, far out of her reach. Her pod had never let her get close enough to get a good look at him. But tonight, as the sharks closed in, she took advantage of a rolling wave to land on his deck and prayed he would help her.

He'd touched her with those strong, suntanned hands, spoken in that gruff, deep voice, and she'd felt more alive in that instant that she ever had before or after the change. She'd been seventeen when she'd gone through the change, and now she was nineteen. She lived her life with the pod, and though she'd had offers to mate, she'd refused because none of those males had felt like the right match for her.

Yet Hudson did. He felt right a thousand different ways. His warm brown eyes and that dark hair falling across his forehead as he reached down to pick her up made her dizzy. She wanted to touch his face, to feel the stubble across his jaw. He was a full ten years older than her, and he was *all* man. He was everything that the human and the siren in her craved. She wanted to know how it felt to lie beneath him, his weight on top of her, as he kissed her, as he claimed her roughly, then tenderly, then again and again until she felt that aching loneliness in her recede like the tide.

She stared forlornly at her tail. The beautiful green-blue scales shone in the moonlight, calling to the sea outside. But her human side was stronger right now. Her human side wanted things it could never have. But if she let the moonlight work its magic, perhaps she could.

Talia surfaced and wiped the water from her eyes

before she concentrated. Her tail began to change, scales receding into human skin. Bones reformed and slid into different places. She moaned softly at the worst of the pain before two slender, shapely legs gleamed in the moonlight in front of her. Wiggling her toes, she bit her lip to hide a shy smile. She was human again until dawn. Talia braced herself on the edge of the tub and stood. Her legs felt a little weak beneath her as she carefully crawled over the tub's side and retrieved a fluffy white bath towel to dry herself. Having grown used to her relative nakedness and her mermaid form, now that she was human, she felt more vulnerable than ever.

She kept her towel wrapped around her and opened the door to the room beyond. The bedroom was dark, but she saw the shape of Hudson's body beneath the sheets. Talia glanced at the windows facing the water and realized that he'd brought the yacht into port while she'd been asleep. The distant lights of the seaside town winked cheerily at her from the balcony of the upper level of the yacht in the master cabin. Glancing back at the man asleep in bed, she knew what she wanted. She wanted Hudson, wanted him so badly it made her ache in strange and secret places. She let the towel fall away and walked toward the bed.

"Hudson..." She whispered his name.

He murmured something softly in his sleep and rolled onto his stomach, one muscular arm stretched out on the bed in her direction. Talia tiptoed across the carpet to the bed and sat down. Her fingers traced a path along his arm, feeling the veins and the muscles. He was so wonderfully warm compared to the sea. She lay down beside him and he curled his arm around her waist, as though they'd been lovers for a lifetime. Her heart clenched in fierce longing, and she felt salty tears sting her eyes. For the first time since her drowning, she fell asleep with a smile upon her lips, and she felt the stirrings of a siren song. Someday soon she would sing to him.

Two

Hudson pulled the warm female body closer to him, sighing as he smelled the sea so strongly it made his heart ache. He used to love the ocean, loved the endless, infinite expanse and depth. It had never made him feel small, but rather as if he was part of something bigger than himself ... until he had lost his parents. The sea had stolen them from him. So why then did the sleek-limbed woman in his bed who smelled of the ocean make him feel at peace rather than full of rage?

He opened his eyes in the moonlight, seeing her, the mermaid, in bed beside him. He glanced at the clock. It was a little after one in the morning. Had he only been a sleep an hour? When had she slipped into bed beside him? As he shifted closer, he felt no scales or fins, only the smooth silky skin of her hip. He moved his fingers down, tracing her thigh, and she lifted her leg up to wrap it around his body. She pressed herself against him, the heat of her sex burning through his briefs. They lay facing each other and her beautiful aquamarine eyes were as luminous as her skin as she stared up at him with shy, hopeful eyes.

"My name is Talia," she whispered.

Talia. A beautiful name for a beautiful woman. He knew this entire situation was insane, but he was too tired to think clearly. Too tired to question the existence of mermaids and whether he was somehow still asleep.

"You have legs." He stroked her thigh, his body impossibly hard, his cock straining against his boxers.

"When the moon is out, I can change my fins into legs." With a sigh she continued. "But by dawn I'll be back in my mermaid form."

"Can all mermaids do this?" he asked, mesmerized.

"No, just me. Others in my pod have other gifts. We aren't the same as those who are born mermaids." She bit her lip and he nearly groaned. He wanted to be the one to bite her lip. But her words sank in properly, prompting other questions.

"Born?"

"Yes, I was made. I was fully human before my accident."

"Your accident?" Hudson's fingers tightened on her thigh, pulling her closer. She was so little compared to him, he realized as he stroked his hands from her knees down to her feet, silently measuring her legs. He was six foot four, and she couldn't have been more than five foot two.

"I was at my senior prom. It was held on a boat, and I fell off, or rather I was *pushed* by another girl. I hit my head on the side of the boat and went under." She glanced away, pain so clear in her blue eyes. "My pod found me and offered me a choice: drown or *change*."

The way she said change held such a note of grave finality to it.

"So I changed."

Hudson's hand stilled. "Wait, your *senior* prom? Fuck, how old are you?" He moved back from her instantly and hurt flashed in her eyes.

"I'm nineteen." Her voice was firm and proud. "Mermaids age just like humans. I didn't die, I *changed*. It's been two years so I'm not biologically seventeen anymore." She stared at him a long moment before adding with the most adult look he'd ever seen on any woman. "I'm *legal*."

He released a breath, not arguing with her. "I can't believe I'm worried about whether a mermaid is legal or not." He sat up and dragged his hands through his hair. "You're still too damn young."

"I'm not, Hudson. And I've been through more than you could ever imagine. Sometimes I feel like I'm a thousand years old, but—" she stopped talking abruptly and rolled onto her back to stare at up at the ceiling.

"But what?" He looked down at her, his body aching as much as his heart when he saw the sorrow on her face.

"I don't fit in with my pod. Never have. I want to be human again, to live a human life and do human things with humans." Her pale skin darkened with a blush.

"What kinds of human things?" he asked.

"Um..." She closed her eyes. "Like ... you know..." She mumbled something beneath her breath.

"Talia, what kind of things?" he pressed. He lay back down on the bed beside her and propped his head in his hand to watch her silent struggle.

"Sex, okay? *Sex*. I never did it in high school with any boy and..."

"Mermaids don't have sex?" He couldn't help his curiosity.

"They do. It's really not that different from being human. The females have slits in their scales where a human woman has her corresponding parts and the males have..." She trailed off again.

"Cocks?" he supplied, barely holding back a chuckle at the look on her face.

"Yes. They slide out when the male is ready for sex, but oh my God, I don't want to talk about this." She crossed her arms over her chest in an adorable shy way.

"But you do *want* to have sex," he said more slowly as

he realized that may be why she was in his bed. "You want sex with me."

She nodded and rolled away to face the windows. The moonlight on the water created little silver ripples on the sides of the boat and off the master bedroom walls as the boat rocked.

A mermaid wanted to have sex with him. But she'd been a human once, a girl who'd had her human life taken from her. It was a selfish thought, but he had no hardship in thinking of making love to her. But first, he tried to stop and acknowledge the entire insanity of this moment.

"You really want me? Not just any guy, but me?" He gripped her shoulder and pulled her to lay flat on the bed so he could see her face. This was not a conversation where she should hide from him.

"I do."

"But why? You don't even know me. I'm just some random man."

"But you aren't," she whispered. "You're *Hudson*."

There it was again, the way she said his name almost like a prayer, as though his name was sacred.

"How do you know my name?" She'd never answered him the first time he'd asked, but he hadn't pressed her. He'd been so worried about her injuries and her being unconscious when he'd first found her.

Those guileless aquamarine eyes met his. "Because my pod sings stories about you."

He held his breath. Mermaids sang songs about him?

"Why?" Something deep inside his chest felt instantly heavy. He knew in that moment he wasn't going to like her answer.

"Because of your parents."

The moonlight seemed to blind him suddenly as the yacht rolled with a bigger wave, and the water illuminated beneath the moon's glow sparkled too brightly to look at.

"My parents? What do you know about them?"

"My pod ... Before I became one of them, years ago, they tried to save your parents, they offered your parents the change but your parents refused. Their last thoughts, last words, were of you as they perished."

Hudson flung himself out of bed and raced to the open balcony doors, rushing into the night air so he could breathe. He clutched the railing of the balcony and drew in lungfuls of air. He wanted to scream, wanted to cry. He wanted to break apart all over again. But he didn't. He bowed his head, resting his forehead against his forearms on the railing as his body quaked. If he had been a continental plate deep beneath the sea, the seismic shift in his soul would've caused a tsunami halfway around the world. His parents' last moments had been to think of him, to speak his name to mermaids who couldn't save them, not without changing them into sea creatures. They'd chosen to drown instead. Why?

"Why did they refuse the change?" he whispered to the water.

"Because loving you from afar would have hurt too much," Talia said. She'd come up beside him. He lifted his head to stare at her. She had wrapped a sheet around her, shielding her nakedness.

"How would you know?" His voice held a note of bitterness in it, but he couldn't help it.

"Because it's easy for even me, a stranger, to watch you from afar and hurt with an aching to be near you. I can't imagine how your parents would have felt, watching you, knowing they couldn't be with you, seeing you live your life as they could when they were human. It would have destroyed them." One of her hands, warm and soft, touched his back and he didn't pull away from the comfort of it.

"To live this life, you are always on the run from the dawn, always staying fathoms below in the crushing darkness of the sea. It's lonely. It's cold."

Needing something, anything to distract himself from the pain that radiated in his heart, he turned to face Talia and gently grasped her hips.

"You want to know what it's like to be with a man?" he asked, his voice low, husky, and rough with pain.

"I want to know what it's like to be with *you*," she corrected.

He slowly backed her up against the glass door of the

balcony and tilted her chin up, staring down at her lush little mouth. He was a bastard for wanting to use her, but he needed this, needed to forget his pain, if only for a few blissful moments.

Hudson slanted his mouth over Talia's, kissing her hard, ruthlessly, giving no quarter and demanding her surrender. Her mouth parted beneath his and she gasped. He slid his tongue between her lips, thrusting slowly, showing her how he would be between her thighs once he got her beneath him. He pulled the sheet away from her body, baring all of her. He knelt in front of her, kissing her belly, then cupping her full breasts, lightly pinching each nipple before he circled his tongue over them. She moaned and dug her hands in his hair, pulling at the strands, and it felt so damn good.

God, she was beautiful, so much so that it almost hurt to touch her. Her pale-pink nipples were ripe berries, eager for his lips. He nipped one, then laved away the sting with his tongue and she made the sweetest sound. The soft crash of waves against the boat and the feel of the night air heightened Hudson's senses as he explored Talia's body. She had full hips and shapely legs, just as mesmerizing as her blue-green tail had been. He flicked his tongue into her navel and moved lower, over her soft abdomen down to the apex between her thighs.

"Spread those pretty legs for me," he growled, and she did. He caught one calf and lifted her leg up and over his shoulder, opening her to him. She leaned back against the balcony door to support herself, her hands falling on his shoulders as he stroked one finger over her labia, tracing and teasing her.

"Hudson," she whimpered, half plea, half demand.

He kissed her inner thigh before his lips moved deeper, his tongue flicking along her sex. She was wet, but not wet enough. She would be soon, given how she was responding. He tasted her fully, thrusting his tongue in and out of her slit, making her shriek in surprise, and he chuckled darkly. He had a little virgin mermaid. This had to be some intense dream. It couldn't possibly be real.

Hudson had always loved going down on a woman, but this was something else. She was so sweet, so utterly addictive, he couldn't get enough. He rubbed the little pearl of her clit with his thumb, and when her legs began to tremble, he knew she was close to coming.

He drew back from her before she came on his tongue and her adorable huff of frustration made him smile. Then he rose and lifted her up in his arms, making her straddle him as he carried her back to the bed. He gently set her on the mattress and followed her down, pinning her beneath him as he used one hand to drag his boxers off. When he kicked them free of his legs, he moved Talia farther up the bed and sat back on his heels, spreading her thighs to stare at her glorious body again. She lay bare before him like a sacrifice to the god Poseidon. But no god of the sea would claim this prize. She was *his*. She dug her hands into the sheet, fisting them as she stared at the hard length of his cock.

He stroked her outer thighs with his palms. "You still want to do this?" It would kill him if she said to stop, but he would.

"Yes, but I'm a little nervous," she admitted, and those beautiful blue eyes grew wide.

"I'll try to go slow, but fuck, honey, this is still going to hurt." He rubbed his shaft in her wetness, coating the tip of his cock before he began to push into her. He met some mild resistance, and she made a slight sound of discomfort.

"Hold on, I'll try to get through the worst of it quickly," he warned, and thrust deep into her. She arched and cried out. He was nearly all the way in. He leaned over her, kissing her lips, distracting her, and after a few minutes, she began to relax and her arms came up around his shoulders, her nails lightly digging into his skin.

"That's it, you're taking me so well, little siren," he murmured in her ear. "Just relax and let me in a little more." He withdrew and thrust more gently this time, managing to go balls-deep inside of her, and she tightened her thighs around his hips with a soft groan.

"It doesn't hurt so much anymore," she whispered.

"Good, it should feel better soon." He rocked against her, listening to the soft sighs she made, and kept his eyes locked on hers for any sign that he might be hurting her. But now he only saw arousal and desire and the flame of some ancient, deep awakening that was a gift for him alone to witness.

The instant she came apart beneath him with that first climax, her eyes closed briefly and her body seized tightly around him, as if afraid to let go. Her inner walls gripped his cock, trying to draw him even deeper, to keep him forever, and damned if he didn't want the same thing. He made love to her slowly, pumping his hips leisurely as he covered her face with tender kisses.

She tilted her chin up, offering herself for anywhere his mouth might want to touch, and he smiled at her sweet, innocent hunger for him. It was so clear she ached for any little bit of affection she could have.

What a lonely little mermaid in the deep dark ocean, he thought.

It made his lips even softer as he sought to give her what she needed. His own climax was close; he could feel that sweet pressure building up in his lower body as he began to move faster, a little harder. When she came a second time with a harsher cry of shock, he unleashed his control and drove into her several more times, his own release blindingly intense as he called out her name hoarsely. He felt his body calm as he released himself inside her and her body held tight, squeezing him in the best way that made him moan. Hudson didn't move for long seconds as his world seemed to wink in and out of existence.

It was only after a moment that sanity returned and he realized a terrible truth. He hadn't used protection. He had always used protection when he slept with someone. What the hell had happened to him? It was too late to do anything now. So he remained inside her, that feeling of pure infinite connection so much more potent somehow than it ever had been with anyone else before.

"Did it feel amazing for you too?" Talia asked in a shy, worried voice. God, this little mermaid was *too* innocent. He nuzzled her nose with his.

"Yeah," he said. He decided to give her the truth. "You are the best I've ever had."

The best sex he ever had? Talia knew she was blushing. Her skin felt hot all over but especially in her face and throat. Maybe he was just being nice. Maybe, but Hudson had a hardness to him, a razor's edge that was frightening sometimes in his intensity, and she somehow knew that lying just to make her feel better didn't fit with this part of his nature. In a lot of ways, he reminded her of an orca whale. Orcas could be helpful and collaborative, or they could be completely terrifying. He was dominating, powerful, and intimidating. But also fiercely protective of what he considered his. By the way he was looking at her now, she felt very much like she belonged to him, and she wanted to.

Finding a mate in the sea wasn't easy, not when mermaids mated for life. The myths painted them as voluptuous creatures seeking to seduce men to their deaths, but that wasn't the full truth. She was a mermaid and she didn't know the first thing about seducing men, and had never wanted to until she'd seen Hudson that first time.

He had dropped anchor out at sea on a sunny summer day and dove off the side of his yacht to cool off. She'd sunk beneath the water, a hundred yards away, watching him, wanting him. She'd never been allowed to get much closer than that, not unless he started to drown. And he never had. He was an excellent swimmer. His arms and legs had powered him through the water almost as well as her tail did. He swam without fear, as though he had nothing to lose, perhaps because he'd already lost his parents.

"What are you thinking about?" he asked. His brown eyes were black in the darkness, reminding her too much of a shark. She didn't feel unsafe with him; not exactly, but she did feel like he was watching her too closely.

"I was thinking about the first time I saw you," she admitted.

"When was that?" he asked, clearly curious.

"Two years ago, just after I turned. It was in the summer, and you would stop your boat to swim out on the open sea. I watched you."

He arched a brow. "Did you spy on me often?"

"I wasn't spying—" she halted her words when she saw him grinning wolfishly down at her, and she realized he was teasing her.

"Okay, I did watch you a lot," she admitted softly. "You were so raw, so powerful for a human. I forgot that men could be like that. I don't spend any time around humans anymore."

"Hmm." He made a sound at the back of his throat that sounded suspiciously like a choked laugh and a hum combined. He was kissing her again and oh God, it was everything she ever wanted. His mouth was on hers, and she forgot about the sea, forgot about the pod, and forgot she wasn't human. Hudson's kiss gave her something she never imagined she would ever have. It gave her herself back. Tears stung her eyes and she clung tighter to him, glad to have his body still connected to hers, to still feel like she was *real*, like she wouldn't float away on the next tide.

Let me stay with you, she silently begged him with her

kiss. *Let me be myself with you. Even if just for a short while.*

When his lips finally lifted from hers, she wanted to cry.

"I don't think you've healed enough to leave. I think you should stay a little while longer, don't you think?" Hudson asked.

"Okay," she replied after pretending to hesitate. Her wish been granted. She would catch hell from her pod later, but swimming away from this man was impossible.

"Good." He kissed her again, longer, slower, as if they had forever.

And oh, how she wished that were true.

THREE

The pain woke Talia. She moaned as her bones knit back together, her skin transforming to scales and her feet stretched into a beautiful tail fin.

"Ahh!" she gasped, unable to keep quiet as the discomfort became too much.

"Talia." Hudson's deep, deliciously rough voice soothed her as his strong arms banded around her.

"Hudson." She burrowed into his hard body, soaking up his warmth. She was always so cold when her fins returned.

"You're changing," he murmured, and she nodded.

"Let's get you into the water." He pulled back the covers to see her long tail stretched out across the bed, so deeply blue and green against the white cotton sheets.

He lifted her up in his arms and carried her into the master bathroom, where he placed her back in the large tub and began running water for her. When he sat down on the edge of the tub, he tested the water's temperature, which made Talia warm all over. He *cared*. This beautiful man, who would have given her the world last night in his arms, actually cared about her. She stared at his face, mesmerized by the marble cut of his features, his sensual mouth, the dark brows that lowered over such brooding intense eyes, and the way those eyes looked back at her as if he saw the girl, not the siren.

"Warm enough?" he asked.

She nodded. She was used to the cold water of the Atlantic, but she would gladly take this warmth and bask in it. She lengthened her tail out, letting the large fluke fin stretch over the lip of the tub so that it brushed Hudson's hip. He reached down to cup some water with his palm and lifted it, dropping the water over the dry scales. She could survive out of the water, but not forever. The moisture felt good, and she moaned as her scales soaked it up. He smiled and trailed wet fingertips over her fluke. It tickled, and she couldn't stop the giggle that escaped her.

"Your fins are as ticklish?" he asked with a laugh of his own.

"Yes," she admitted with a blush. No one ever touched her tail so intimately. With anyone else she would have felt strange and uncomfortable, but with Hudson it felt wonderful and right. She wanted his hands all over her.

"You mind if I touch you?" he asked. "I don't want to do anything you don't want me to."

"You can touch me," she assured him. She wanted him to. *Desperately.*

His fingers on her fin continued to stroke her, and she luxuriated in the touch.

"Tell me more about the pods, about being a mermaid."

"You really want to know?"

Hudson chuckled and faint laugh lines bracketed his mouth. "Hell yes. I just found out mermaids are real. I want to know *everything.*"

As the water in the tub rose up over her hips, she told him everything she knew about mermaids and life under the sea. She told tales of its beauty, its danger, its vastness, and its majesty. He listened intently to every word, only interrupting every now and then with questions.

"And before, when you were human?"

Those memories hurt, probably because they were the ones she cherished the most.

"Most mermaids who change, not the ones who are born, learn to forget their human lives and go forward with their new life in the sea. But I think I was too young to understand what I was giving up."

"You were just a kid," he solemnly agreed.

"I had a family, had friends, I had a..." She choked on the last word that she couldn't say.

"You had a life," he finished for her.

"Yes."

"A pretty mermaid who doesn't want to be one," he mused.

"Almost poetic, isn't it? Most girls dream of being mermaids at one point in their lives, and here I am complaining about it."

"I think it's heartbreaking," Hudson said, his gaze solemn as he reached forward and cupped her chin. "I wish I could fix it. I wish I could give you what you want."

Through salty tears, she smiled up at him. "But you have ... you gave me *you*."

Damn, this woman ... this mermaid, was killing him with her sweetness.

You gave me you. How could he be a gift? He was just a man, a very flawed man with a heart as broken as hers.

He couldn't resist leaning over and brushing his lips over hers in a slow, deep kiss. He couldn't get enough of her now that he'd touched her and talked to her. She was fascinating inside and out. Her lips were petal soft, and he flicked his tongue against hers until she opened her mouth to his. Then he thrust his tongue in her mouth in a slow rhythm, reminding them both of last night.

It was just after dawn, and he would have to wait for the moon to rise to take her again. It was torture and he couldn't help but kiss her for long moments, just have an excuse to keep touching her. Was it because she was a mermaid? Or because she was just Talia, a woman who had lost so much, like he had, and he felt connected to her in a way he never had with anyone else before?

When their mouths parted, he relished the way she kept her eyes closed, her lips pursed as if she still tasted his kiss after he moved away. Those lush lips of hers curved in entrancing smile as she opened her eyes.

"I don't have any tours booked for a few days, why don't we sail over to Wreckers' Cove and have a picnic on the shore?" he asked. Wrecker's Cove was a lovely little cove inside the larger bay that most tourists didn't know about.

"Really? I'd love that. No one will see us?"

"No, no one really goes to Wreckers' Cove. It's not easy to reach by car and you need a dinghy to reach it by boat. So we should have some privacy. I think would be nice have some time together." He grinned. "Stay here. I'm going to run into town for some picnic supplies."

She laughed. "I can't exactly go anywhere." She waved a hand at her tail.

"True." He chuckled. "I'll hurry back." He leaned down to give her one more hard, quick kiss before he went into his bedroom and dressed so he could leave the boat.

Once he stepped off the deck of the *Splash*, he crossed the docks and headed for the nearest grocery store. The sleepy little town of Shell Harbor was an ideal place to live, with adorable little coastal houses, cozy pubs, and nice restaurants. He'd lived here his whole life except for when he went away to college, and he had no regrets. The people here were like family to him.

As he entered the grocery store, someone called out his name.

"Hudson!" A man's rich baritone boomed. "You're early for supplies." John Porter, the grocer, said. He had boxes stacked up on a rolling cart and was coming down the aisle toward Hudson. "You usually come in on Saturdays."

"I know," Hudson said. "I decided to have a picnic today and I didn't have any decent food on the boat since I don't have any tours until next week."

"Well, load up and Maggie will check you out." Maggie was John's wife.

"Thanks." Hudson grabbed a basket at the end of the nearest aisle and started shopping. Not sure what mermaids ate, he got a mix of things from peanut butter and jelly, to sandwich meat, to chicken salad. He didn't pick up any seafood. He had a funny feeling that she'd had plenty of fish in the last two years, and he wanted to give her a taste of human food again. He met Maggie at the front of the store to check out, and she pestered him about his upcoming tours. She was like a favorite aunt, and always wanted to make sure he had plenty of supplies.

"Need any more milk?" she asked, looking over his selections. He had a gallon of milk already.

"I'm think I'm good, thanks Maggie."

"Hudson?" A familiar voice halted him in the middle of filling his basket with food and he turned away from the cashier. His uncle stood there smiling. "You have a tour today?" Jason nodded at the groceries in Hudson's arms.

"No, I just thought I'd have a picnic today."

His uncle's gaze lit with interest. "Oh? With who?"

Shit ... He hadn't expected to run into his uncle. "Uh, just myself."

Jason's eyes narrowed slightly. "You okay, kid?"

Kid. He and Jason were only eight years apart. His grandparents had had Jason late in life when Hudson's father was sixteen. Ever since Hudson had lost his parents, Jason had gone from being almost an older brother to a surrogate father.

"Yeah, I just figured after the last couple of months of back-to-back tours that I would take a couple of days for myself."

"Makes sense," Jason said. "The restaurant has been

running me ragged. I'm looking forward to the end of tourist season ending in a month as crazy as it sounds. I might take some time off myself." Jason's restaurant, the Black Spot Pub, a fun pirate-themed restaurant, overlooked the bay and was always packed with tourists and even locals.

Jason suddenly grinned. "Feel free to bring your girl by the restaurant tonight if you want."

"My girl?" Hudson choked on the two words.

"Yeah, you have that same expression on your face as that summer when you were sixteen and used to sneak out to see that girl visiting from New York. Your parents knew you were slinking off to see her." Jason laughed. "You know you're not sixteen anymore. You don't have to hide dates and worry about curfew."

"True." Hudson chuckled. "If there was a girl, maybe I'd bring her, but the truth is, I just need some time to unwind, that's all."

"Uh huh." His uncle clearly didn't believe him. "My offer still stands, if you want to come by," Jason called over his shoulder before he grabbed a cart and started shopping for groceries.

Hudson quickly paid Maggie and darted back out to the street. He had to get his boat out of the docks fast. The last thing he needed was Jason coming aboard the *Splash* to visit in hopes of catching sight of some girl and instead discovering a mermaid. His uncle had been through too much when it came to the accident and the storm that had killed the man's brother and sister-in-law. He didn't want his uncle suffering anymore. Hudson returned to the boat and put away the groceries in the kitchenette before he went to check on Talia.

His little mermaid was humming softly as she lounged in the bathtub, splashing water and giggling.

There was a strange vibration in the air as he listened to the haunting harmonies she made as she hummed. His vision started to blur; everything except Talia seem to slip out of focus. He was moving before he could think twice, and knelt by the bathtub.

She stopped humming when she saw him. "Hudson!" she exclaimed with a delighted grin.

He grabbed her by the nape of her neck and pulled her mouth toward his. She moaned as he captured her lips and kissed her hard, hungrily and with such wild desperation. Her lingering humming seemed to vibrate through his veins.

She curled her arms around his neck, and he stroked his palms over her wet back and arms and then slid his hands between their bodies so he could cup her gorgeous, full breasts. His body was hard, so hard it fucking hurt, but there was a tender sweetness in the way she made him ache for her. She pressed herself into his palms, whimpering in soft encouragement for him to knead her breasts and play with her sensitive nipples.

Slowly the desperate need to possess her faded, along with the lulling haze of her siren song in his head. But the passion he felt for Talia wasn't fading away. It continued to burn steadily like a hearty fire in the darkest coldest winter of his heart. He knew then that what he was feeling for her, this woman ... this siren, was not influenced by the power of her song, but something deeper, more ancient than the sea that rocked the ship beneath their feet. She sighed his name as he finally let them both come up for air.

"Hi," Talia breathed shyly, her cheeks turning an adorable shade of pink. God, she had no idea of the effect she had on him.

"Hi," he echoed, smiling at her as he continued to hold her even though they both leaned awkwardly against the bathtub that separated them.

"I got us lunch. I'll steer us into the cove and then come get you when we're ready to go ashore."

Talia held still as Hudson carried her from the bathtub to the ship's back deck half an hour later. There was a flat area on the back of the boat that allowed swimmers to slip

off the side or climb down a ladder into the water without
having to jump.

"You ready?" he asked her. She answered with a nod.

He put her down so that she sat on the edge of the
boat and her tail dropped in the water, then he crouched
beside her.

"I'll meet you in the shallows."

"Okay." She grasped his shoulder and pulled his head
down for a kiss and he smiled against her lips. Talia
stroked a fingertip over his mouth before she plunged into
the sea to swim toward the shore. She rode the waves into
the shallows and dragged herself through the sand, stop-
ping just where the water lapped at her lower tail and
fluke. Hudson used a small dinghy to take towels, blan-
kets, and the food bag ashore. He carried the supplies to a
place far away from the water so their picnic wouldn't get
washed away, and then he stripped down to his swim
trunks. After that, he came and collected her from the
shallows, placed her gently on a blanket, and wrapped a
towel around her shoulders like a cape to keep her warm.

Talia's mouth ran dry at the sight of his tan skin in the
sunlight and the beautiful way his muscles moved when
he bent to set up their picnic on the soft sand. They had
plenty of concealment thanks to the tall, wheat colored
grasses that lined the upper shore past the edge of Wreckers' Cove.

When Hudson showed her the meal he'd prepared, she practically squealed in delight.

"Peanut butter!" God, she had missed peanut butter and jelly sandwiches. She ate two full sandwiches before snacking on the Cheetos he'd brought. She'd told him last night that peanut butter and Cheetos had been two of her favorite foods and that she missed them terribly, and he'd remembered. Again, his thoughtfulness, even in so small a thing, made her heart clench. She licked the cheesy crumbs off her fingers and blushed as she realized Hudson was watching her. His own plate was clean of food and his eyes were hot as they fixed on her.

"God, you're beautiful," he whispered.

Sorrow pricked her heart as a fear she'd been trying to ignore surfaced. "It's the siren, not me, who you're attracted to." She'd seen it so often her pod sisters and brothers. Their singing, even their humming, could affect humans and make them feel desire when normally they might not. Her appearance had altered ever so slightly to have some sort of supernatural glow that drew humans in. Her hair, once streaked with faint gold now was a rich dark brown that enhanced the glow of her paler skin, while her once gray eyes were now a bright aquamarine blue.

He slowly shook his head. "No, it isn't. I can actually feel the difference. Like when you hum or sing it makes me feel fuzzy, but right now I'm seeing you clearly, and

I'm thinking clearly. You're beautiful, Talia. Your laugh, your smile, the way you won't give up even when life takes away everything."

His words humbled her. "I didn't know giving up was possible."

His eyes shadowed with old pain. "It's possible. Lots of people give up. I had until you washed up on my boat."

His words gave her heart such a fluttering hope she was almost too afraid to speak lest she break the spell that held them together.

"Take me to the water," she whispered.

"You want to leave?" he asked.

She shook her head. "I want you to swim with me." She held out her hand and he clasped it in his own, pressing his lips to her fingertips. Then he carried her to the water.

She had a lot of trouble moving on land without feet, but once she hit the water, she wriggled through the waves, easily moving out to where the retreating waves turned into smooth, rolling hills, and Hudson followed.

He was tall enough to stand chest-deep in the water. She came to him, wrapping her arms around his neck and kissing him. She was careful not to knock his feet out from under him with her tail as she moved it gently back and forth in the water. He growled softly in delight, catching her by the waist and holding her against him. He lightly threaded his fingers in her hair, holding her head still so he could kiss more ruthlessly. The man could kiss better than she ever imagined anyone could. Even though she had barely any experience before Hudson, she knew he was a master of kisses. The things he did with his tongue were marvelous, and she never wanted him to stop. He could make a single kiss feel like it contained the entire universe.

"I could kiss you forever," he whispered, his eyes so soft as he stared her. She held on tighter.

"I'd let you," she replied, earning a warm smile from him. "I want to show you my world. Come with me." She pointed to the rock outcropping that edged part of the cove on their left. "There's a grotto under that group of rocks, one with plenty of air and room to stand up, did you know that?"

"What? No, can I reach it?"

"If you hold your breath and take my hand."

He let go of her body but recaptured one of her hands as they both swam toward the rocks. When they got closer, she halted, her tail moving in the water to keep her upright.

"Take a big breath and don't let go of me." She waited for him to inhale, and they both dove beneath the surface. She kept a tight grip on his hand and swam harder, moving her tail vigorously so she could get him through the murky waters and into the safety of the grotto. When they broke the surface, a pale shaft of light came through an opening in the rocks above to let them see the grotto.

Hudson slicked his hair back with his hands and glanced around as he trod water.

"Holy shit, I had no idea this was here."

Talia grinned. "I come here a lot to have time away from the pod." She swam toward the rock ledge that was only an inch or so above the surface of the water.

"Does it flood when the tides come in?" Hudson joined her, pulling himself up to sit on the rock next to her.

"Nope. Crazy, right?" She scooted closer to him, wanting to feel his warmth now that she was once again cold from the waters of the Atlantic.

"It's a beautiful sanctuary," Hudson said and put an arm around her shoulders.

She leaned into him, both silently watching the water as the shaft of light illuminated the eddies of the sea, which flashed with glints of silver.

"I wonder if we would've met..." he mused softly and rubbed his cheek along the top of her head.

"Hmm?" She sighed, half listening as he continued.

"If you had never fallen off that boat, if you never changed. Would we have ever crossed paths?"

"I don't know. I had a scholarship to go to Princeton," she said. "I don't know if I would have come back except to visit my parents." She'd planned on studying microbiology and learning everything she could about the world around her. Those dreams had died when she'd realized her choice to change had taken her future away.

"Are they still here? Your parents?"

She shook her head. "They moved. They decided it would be better to live farther inland. It took me months of hiding beneath the docks near some of the restaurants before I finally heard them speaking one night. They came to dinner at one of the nice steakhouses and were discussing the sale of my family's house. They both sounded so hollow. Mom just wanted to move, and Dad was so quiet. I don't think he said more than a dozen words the entire dinner. By the time they finished eating, I knew they would be leaving forever. I whispered my goodbye and let out a song from my lips. It drew them to look out over the harbor and I had one last chance to see their faces." Briny tears coated her face, and she closed her eyes as Hudson wiped them away with his callused fingertips.

"You're killing me, sweetheart," he murmured, and then gently pushed her back on the smooth ledge of rocks. She lay on her back and he lay down beside her. He leaned over Talia, pressing soft kisses to her mouth, her cheeks, her jaw and then her neck. Her body burned with desire, and she clutched his arms, needing to hold onto him to keep herself from floating away.

When his mouth nuzzled one bare breast, she moaned

his name in a desperate plea. His other hand cupped her other breast, squeezing gently while he suckled.

Sharp pangs of pleasure shot through her body until she felt like she had a wild raging fever in her blood.

"Can I touch you?" he asked between carnal kisses on her breasts.

"Touch me?" she echoed. He *was* touching her.

"Lower. I don't know if you like to be touched there while you're in mer form..." He glided one palm over her scale-covered hip, sending a fluttering of sensations across her skin. The scales reacted just as powerfully to his touch as her human skin did. The sensations were somehow different, but just as wonderful.

"Y—yes," she shivered as his fingertips stroked the scales so lightly yet with such a powerful purpose of seduction.

"Show me where," he urged.

She grasped his wrist and guided his hand toward the hidden slit at the front of her body that was close to where the apex of her thighs and mound would be in her human body. She showed him how she wanted to be touched. The moment his fingers penetrated her she groaned in sheer, lustful agony. His mouth returned to hers, his kisses voracious as he listened to her sounds. He touched her in the most intimate of places and her body quaked as the grotto rang with her cries of pleasure. She lay panting beside him for long moments before she realized he was staring at her with a utterly male look of satisfaction.

"You're so beautiful when you come apart in my arms," he said. "So beautiful it hurts."

Talia couldn't resist smiling at his words. They emboldened her. She pushed him to lie flat on the rock ledge and she slid over him, kissing his chest and working her way down his stomach to where his swim trunks hid his lower body. She tugged at the waistband of the trunks, and he lifted his hips, letting them slide down. His cock jutted upward eagerly, and Talia stared at it in fascination. She'd heard about women giving head, but had never done it. Curiously, she grasped his thick shaft in one hand and he moaned.

"Fuck, yes, touch me," Hudson growled in encouragement.

She bent her head, brushing her lips over his cock and he cursed again, which made her giggle. It was clear he liked what she was doing. She flicked her tongue along his erection, exploring him, and his hands formed fists at his sides. A few minutes later, Talia finally drew him into her mouth, and her body hummed, delighted by his response. His face was flushed, and his hips eagerly lifted an inch or two as he tried to push his cock deeper into her mouth.

"Yes." He uttered the word as a half-command, half-plea as she started to suck him. She let him bob in and out of her mouth while she gripped the base of the shaft in her hand to hold him. He was too big to fit even halfway in her mouth, but she tried to take as much of him as deeply as possible. She could feel he was close to coming; his thighs shook and his face was twisted with the torturous pleasure of near-release. But before she could experience him releasing inside of her mouth, he pushed up and his cock slipped from her startled lips.

He rolled her beneath him, pinning her down. She gasped as he thrust into her suddenly, his shaft pushing into her slit, and she cried out his name. It felt just as good as when she'd been in human form, yet it felt different. He surged deep into her body, his hard cock pushing into her channel in a steady rhythmic thrusting. Hudson gazed down at her, taking what he wanted from her, his face hard with hunger, which only made her burn with an intense arousal. The ache in her womb only grew stronger. He was the star of a secret thousand fantasies she'd had, the helpless mermaid caught by handsome sailor who plundered her with his body, claiming her forever with a look of pure desire in his eyes.

"Mine." Hudson breathed the single word almost in warning.

Yes. She was his. He'd been the one to lure her out of the water rather than she to lure him into the sea.

Hudson braced himself above her, staring down into her eyes as he fucked her almost without mercy, and she felt her body explode atom by atom before binding itself back together. He shouted her name, his body vibrated, and she felt something warm fill her deep inside. Her inner walls quaked, and she clenched her muscles to hold him inside her for a long moment.

His eyes softened as he continued to gaze at her. He didn't need to say anything; so many emotions showed so clearly on his face. But when he did speak it, changed her life.

"Don't go back to the sea. Stay with me in Shell Harbor."

Four

Hudson knew he had surprised Talia by asking her to stay with him. Hell, he had surprised himself, but he wouldn't take the words back. Talia was his. By some strange twist of fate, he had found someone to love with his whole heart.

He didn't feel empty, not when he held Talia in his arms. She had lost her world and her human life. If he could give her even half of it back, fuck, he would do *anything* for her. Some tiny part of him warned him he was probably thinking with the wrong head, but he loved her. He genuinely loved to talk to her, to sit quietly with her, to just *be* with her. He'd never felt that way with anyone before.

"You want me to stay?" Her lower lip quivered, and he

couldn't resist kissing her so that he could nibble that trembling lip with his teeth. He was still buried inside her, all too aware that he'd made love to her in her mer form, but it had worked. They'd fit together in all the ways that had mattered, and he'd given her such an intense pleasure that she'd started to hum with that siren song as she'd climaxed. That had filled him with unspeakable joy.

He could touch her, please her, make love to her no matter her form, that meant he could give her what she needed. She'd already stolen his heart, now she had his body and soul, and he wouldn't deny it. Losing his parents had taught him that life was short, precious, and lived only once. Now that he had Talia, he never wanted to lose her.

"I want you to," he confirmed. "Live with me, *be mine.*"

She stared up at him with those piercing blue eyes so full of sweet innocence. "Will you be mine too?" she asked.

"Yes, God yes, sweetheart," he promised, and nuzzled her nose with his before kissing her by brushing of his mouth over hers.

"But how?" she asked.

"Do you need ocean water?" He rolled their bodies to lay side-by-side and he pulled out of her, carefully fixing his swim trunks back into place.

"No, but it would be nice to get to the sea every

couple of days." Her ties to the water couldn't be fully broken.

"My house is close to the beach. Funnily enough, I have a decent pool in my backyard. When the moon is out, we can walk to the yacht, and when you're back in your fins, we can take the ship out and stay at sea as long as you want to. I have to schedule a few tours each month, but we can just use that as a few days for you to get some ocean time with your pod."

She seemed to consider it. "My pod might be a little angry, but..." Tears clung to her lashes. "But being with you makes me feel real again. I had become a shadow, and I don't ever want to be a shadow again."

"You deserve to have a full life and I will do all that I can to give you one," he promised.

"Thank you." She snuggled closer to him, pressing her body against his as he wrapped his arms around her. Her large, lovely pale-blue tail fin, which was a lighter color than the rest of her tail, dip in and out of the water playfully, creating little splashes. For some reason that delighted him; he loved the mermaid side of her as much as the human.

"Want to have another sandwich?" he asked. He wanted to make sure she ate enough. Given that the shark attack marks on her skin were now just pink stripes, he realized that she'd healed fast, and he guessed that her higher metabolism would therefore mean she needed more food.

"I would never turn down another PB&J sandwich." She giggled and the sound filled his heart with cottony warmth.

"Good, then let's go."

They slipped off the ledge of the pool and she took his hand to lead him back out of the grotto. They broke the surface outside, once more back in the pull of the tide, and he tugged her close for a kiss as they let the waters gently carry them toward the shore. They lay in the shallow water in the sand, feeling the small waves lap at their lower bodies as they kissed. The sound of a rifle cocking sent shockwaves through Hudson, pulling him out of the secret world he and Talia shared.

"Kid, back away from the creature and come toward me." Jason's voice came from behind them.

Hudson shielded Talia with his body as he sat up in the sand to face Jason. Jason stood with a rifle aimed at them, his eyes cold and hard as he looked only at Talia. It took him a moment to realize what he was seeing. His uncle as standing on the beach just inches from the water...he'd braved his fear because he'd worried about Hudson.

"Uncle ... she's not—" Hudson raised his palms in a gesture to calm the other man. If he could just explain to his uncle what had happened everything would be okay.

"A monster? She'll drown you, Hudson. Move away from her before she drags you into the water."

"Jason, she's not going to hurt me. If you would just put the gun down..." Hudson slowly got to his feet, still moving to block Talia who sat up and had her arms wrapped around herself in a terrified hug.

"I told you ... been telling you for years ... they killed your parents."

"No, they didn't." Hudson took a cautious step toward his uncle, pulling Jason's gaze away from Talia. Good. He wanted his uncle's focus on him.

"You weren't there kid, you didn't see. I tried so goddamn hard to get the cabin door open, but the water pressure sealed it shut. The ship was going down, and..." Jason's hands began to shake. "They screamed and beat at the door and there was nothing I could do ... God, your dad... I couldn't get to him..."

Jason swallowed hard, pain fracturing his voice as his gaze shifted back to Talia. "And *they* were waiting ... waiting for us, but they didn't get me." His gaze hardened on Talia with fear and despair. "And they'll sure as hell won't get you." Jason growled and lifted the gun a few inches.

Hudson reacted without thinking and stepped more fully in front of Talia as she moved back in the shallows. A split second later the gun fired. Talia's soft cry made Hudson spin, fearing to see her in pain. If anything happened to her, he'd never survive it. She meant to much to him now, too much. As he spun, pain, such god-awful pain, exploded through his left side. He grunted and stared down at his stomach. Blood welled up from a place on the left side below his ribs. Talia was all right...but he wasn't. The realization rumbled about his head far too slowly for him to catch hold of it and understand it fully.

"Hudson!" His uncle caught him as he struggled, staggered, and fell to his knees. "Shit, I didn't meant to....oh god, please," his uncle's voice wavered with agony.

"Hudson, no..." Talia's voice, so sweet, reached his ears as he felt himself being laid down on the sand. The two people he loved most in this world were on either side of him. Not fighting each other, but worried about him. He wanted to tell them not to worry, but damn...he could barely talk, could barely think. So much pain ... was this what it felt like to die?

"No, please no..." Talia's face blacked out the sun as she leaned over him.

"Love you, little siren ... love you," he murmured drowsily before his eyes closed.

"Oh my God!" Jason gasped, his face white as coral that had been bleached by the sun.

"He's going to die unless we do something," Talia whispered to herself, trying to stay calm. She could save him. She could change him. No, she couldn't do that, not to Hudson. She could never take his life from him the way hers had been stolen.

"Jason, call 911." She shook Hudson's uncle's shoulder. The man blinked at her. She nodded. "Do it now."

"How do you know what the hell 911 is?" he demanded of her.

"Because I was human once. Just do it." She shoved him hard and he dug through his pockets looking for his phone. Talia cradled Hudson's head in her lap and waited, her heart beating so hard and so loud she felt bruised and deafened by it. But as she heard Jason talking to the paramedics, she knew they wouldn't be here soon enough. Hudson's breathing was too shallow and too slow.

"Jason, we're losing him!" she called out. Jason ran back to her, kneeling on the sand to examine his nephew.

"You've got to hurry!" he practically shouted the paramedics. "He's dying! Come on, kid. Stay with us."

A distant singing came across the waves and Talia looked out over the water behind them. A woman's face appeared past the breaking surf. Her sister, Isabel.

"Izzy!" she cried out to the other mermaid. "Izzy, *please* help me."

Isabel swam closer and joined them in the shallows. Her gaze flicked to Jason, who stared at her in fear and fascination as he took in the long blue tail that stretched out behind her.

"Will he agree to the change?" Isabel asked Talia.

"I can't make him do that. It wouldn't be fair." Talia wiped tears from her cheeks. Isabel's dark hair fell across her face as she studied Hudson, then she let out a deep sigh. "I can save him without changing him."

"You can?" Talia clung to a foolish wellspring of hope like a liferaft.

"Yes, I was saving this for you, but..." Isabel leaned over Hudson and placed her lips on his, breathing into his mouth while she hummed softly.

Notes of her siren song wove around them, and Talia gasped as she felt something still human inside her respond to the power of Isabel's song. Power, pure and deep from the sea filled the water and sand around them with an electric charge. Hudson's body seized, his muscles tensing and his lungs heaving upward as his eyes flew open. Isabel sank weakly back into the sand, her pale skin even more white than before, making her look almost translucent. Her fins wilted and she looked ready to collapse.

"Izzy?" Talia touched her sister's arm in worry but Izzy shied away.

"Take care of your human, little sister," Isabel said

before she slipped away into the deeper water and disappeared.

Talia turned back to Hudson, who stared at her in dazed confusion.

"Talia ... what happened? I felt like I went somewhere far away. Did I leave?" He sounded so confused, so worried. Jason pushed him back down to the sand when Hudson tried to sit up.

"Hold on kid, I need to see your wound." He wiped the bloody area with a bit of one of the beach towels from the picnic. It was smooth, no evidence of a gunshot having ever been there.

"What the..." Jason didn't finish his thought. He just stared at Hudson's stomach.

Hudson placed a hand to the place where the wounded been, his brows drawing together as he seemed to start remembering what had happened.

"Where's Talia?" his fear spiked.

"Here." She put a hand on his shoulder, and he turned, pulling her into his arms, his body shaking as he held onto her. He kissed her cheek, holding her tight enough that she could barely breathe.

"You're okay. Thank God, you're okay," he murmured over and over.

"Somebody explain what the hell I'm seeing?" Jason demanded. "You're cuddling a damn mermaid."

Hudson sighed against her neck and kept his little mermaid on his lap as he faced his uncle.

"Well, first thing you have to know is that mermaids are real."

Jason glared at him. "I've been saying that for *years*."

"But you didn't know that the pod that visits our harbor aren't here to hurt us."

Talia listened to Hudson's heartbeat more than his words as he explained what had happened to his parents. Jason sank down to the sand, his face washed once more of all color as he learned the truth.

"The mermaids were trying to *save* me?"

Hudson nodded. "They aren't allowed to intervene, but they were ready to offer you the chance to change into one of them instead of dying. But the Coast Guard found you before you succumbed to the elements."

Jason dragged his hands through his hair, staring out across the water for a long while before he focused on Hudson again.

"So this little one," he nodded at Talia. "She's yours?"

"Yes," Hudson replied. "She's *mine*."

"So does this mean you're going to be living on the boat all the time now?" A look of loneliness crossed his uncle's face.

"Not all the time. She can form legs when the moon is out, which gives us some time to be together as humans.

And with a pool at the house ... we're going to try to find a way to make it work."

"Huh." Jason stared now at the abandoned shotgun and then suddenly tensed as ambulance sirens sounded in the distance. "Shit. You need to get this out of here. Take it." He passed the gun to Hudson. "Sink it in the harbor."

"Give it to me, I'll put it in the grotto." Talia took the gun from Hudson and dove into the waves before either man could stop her.

Talia quickly swam toward the grotto and deposited the gun on the ledge. When she got back out to the open water, she found Hudson had rowed back to his yacht, and was finishing tying up his dinghy. He helped her up on the back of his boat and she wrapped her arms around the silver handles connected to the short ladder that dropped into the water. It would give her a way to hold onto the boat once he started the engines. Within a few minutes after raising anchor, they were out to sea and far away from shore. When Hudson stopped the yacht far from Wreckers' Cove, he came down to sit beside her, dropping his legs into the sea as they both stared at the endless blue before them.

"What will your uncle do?"

"He's going to tell the cops and paramedics he hallucinated. It wouldn't be the first time, according to them. He's said that mermaids are real in quite a few public places while he had some panic attacks. So the local police department knows he has some issues."

"Poor Jason," Talia whispered.

"At least he knows the truth and he won't try to hurt you," Hudson said with a sigh.

"So you won't mind dating a mermaid?"

"Mind? One is the love of my life, and another saved my life. I didn't dream that, did I?"

"Nope, you didn't dream it. Isabel, my pod sister, saved you. Jason and I thought you weren't going to make it, but something happened as she hummed... I've never heard anything like that before. It affected me, and siren songs don't usually do that, not once I changed into a mermaid."

"Maybe we can ask her about it." Hudson pointed out to sea and Talia glimpsed the distant figure of Isabel in the water.

"Izzy!" she called out, but her sister had already spotted them and was swimming their way. She paused a few feet from the back of the boat and watched them warily. She was still so very pale and moved weakly through the water. Talia was glad her sister had left the harbor.

"Izzy, this is Hudson."

The other mermaid nodded in greeting at him.

"Thank you for saving my life," Hudson said and curled an arm around Talia's shoulders.

"You're welcome." Izzy's eyes settled on Hudson. "He's the one you choose?" she asked Talia.

Talia's throat constricted. Her sister knew that if she chose a human as her mate, she wouldn't be fully welcome in the pod anymore. They weren't against humans, but it was more that trying to bridge the two worlds didn't work. There was too much risk of bringing danger to the pod, so was better to choose and leave one or the other behind. And that meant saying goodbye to Izzy for possibly a long time.

"You, human, treat my sister like the pearl she is, understand?" Isabel warned.

Hudson answered with a solemn reply. "She's everything to me, and I'll take care of her."

His answer seemed to satisfy Isabel. "Give me one more hug, Talia, then I must go."

Talia slid off the back of the boat into the water where she embraced the woman who was as real a sister to her as anyone she'd ever known.

"I love you, Izzy."

"I love you too Talia. Be happy with your gorgeous man." Isabel smiled, and even though sorrow showed in her eyes, she looked happy for Talia.

"Will you visit if the pod lets you?"

"Yes, if I can," Isabel promised her. They hugged once more and Isabel stroked Talia's hair, still smiling sadly. Then she let go of Talia and dove beneath the surface, her tailfin splashing once before she vanished from sight.

Talia wiped away more tears. It felt like she'd been crying most of the day. When she pulled herself back together, she swam toward the yacht and Hudson pulled her onto his lap, holding her close as they both sat for a long while in silence.

"I didn't know you'd have to leave your family. It's not too late to change your mind," Hudson murmured in her ear.

"You don't want me to stay?" Icy pain dug claws in her chest.

"I do, sweetheart, so much. It would kill me to lose you, but your happiness matters more than anything else to me."

She leaned into him once more, curling her arms around his neck and hugging him.

"I choose *you*. I'll always choose you."

Hudson cupped her cheek, stroking her lips with the pad of his thumb.

"We'll make this work. I know we will."

She smiled through happy tears now. "Yes, we will." She'd been human once and if she could claim even a small part of it back with Hudson, she would do whatever she had to. She placed a hand over his stomach, the faint smears of partially washed-away blood remained on his pure, undamaged skin. Isabel had used her gift from the sea to save Hudson's life. Isabel had never told anyone what her gift really was; she'd only said it was incredibly hard to use.

Talia lifted her head to his. "Kiss me, Hudson," she pleaded.

His eyes softened and his lips curved into a smile that promised love deeper than any sea.

"For forever, if I can," he replied, and pressed his lips to hers in a kiss sweeter and more tempting than any siren song.

EPILOGUE

One month later ...

    Talia slipped out of bed half an hour before the moon vanished from the sky. She'd be back in her fins by then, but for now, she enjoyed the chance to be on her feet for a while. Hudson still lay sleeping in their bed on the *Splash*; she didn't want to wake him. There was a part of the siren in her that still liked to have time alone to just sit and stare at the sea.

As she walked across the deck barefoot, she moved carefully, noting her tenderness. Hudson had made love to her so vigorously last night that she was deliciously sore between her thighs. A sleepy smile curved her lips as she walked down to the lower deck by the back of the boat. Moonlight danced along the surface of the sea, making silvery patterns so bright they almost blinded her.

So far, she and Hudson had managed to survive this dance between fins and feet each day. They had even crafted a story in town about her only coming out at night due to skin sensitivity. Luckily, the locals believed it. No one seemed to recognize Talia as the young woman who'd drowned on her prom night two years before. Perhaps it was because her eyes were such a bright blue now, when they'd used to be a pale gray, and it was enough for people to forget they had once known a girl like her.

She leaned on her forearms on the railing and watched the sea. She hadn't missed her pod, but she missed Isabel so much it was a physical ache. As if the sea could hear her thoughts, Isabel's face emerged in the water close by.

"Izzy!" She rushed toward the flat landing area at the back of the yacht where she could be closest to the water. Her sister met her there and pulled herself up onto the ledge using the silver ladder. Talia threw her arms around her sister.

"How is your human?" Talia asked as her tail moved slowly back and forth in the water. If she'd been human, she would have been gently kicking her legs.

"Wonderful, simply wonderful. Things are working out." Talia assured her sister.

"You love him," Isabel observed.

"I do. And he loves me." She blushed at the memory of Hudson murmuring those words as they'd cooked dinner together last night. She'd been stirring pasta in a pot while he'd been washing lettuce for a salad, and he'd simply leaned over, kissed her cheek and spoken those three words in her ear.

He had said it every day since she'd chosen to stay with him, and she said it back to him as easily as breathing. And she was *happy*. Yes, the change hurt, and she hated not having legs most of the time, but loving Hudson and him loving her made the little daily struggles worth it. Hudson was even talking about ways to remodel the house to build some shallow water features that would connect several rooms, so she could swim through parts of the house. It was going to be a complicated remodel, and far too expensive, but he was so excited when he showed her the design plans, and she didn't want to discourage him.

"I never had the chance to thank you for saving Hudson's life."

"You're welcome," Isabel said and cupped Talia's cheek. "You were never meant for the sea. I can't give you back the last two years, but I can give you a future." She stared deeply into Talia's eyes.

"What do you mean?"

"I never told you about my gift," Isabel said.

"I know. I didn't want to push you to tell me." Talia had sensed it was painful to talk about. Not all gifts were gifts, some were *curses*.

"I have a kiss that restores whatever I desire, whether

it's energy, life or joy. I have but to concentrate on it and then hum while giving my kiss."

A kiss that could restore anything. Was that possible?

"Talia, I can restore your humanity."

"My humanity?" That meant her sister could take the siren part of her away?

"Yes, you would be fully human again."

"What does it cost?" Talia wouldn't let hurt sister get hurt, not even for that.

"I will be weak for a while, but the pod has come to protect me." She pointed at the distant shapes of mermaids waiting in the distance.

"You'd do that for me?" Being vulnerable and weak in the ocean was dangerous; it could get Isabel killed if she wasn't careful. And yet she'd done it before, for Hudson. Isabel truly loved her. "Izzy, I already owe you for Hudson's life. How could I ever repay you for more?"

"There is no debt to someone you love." Isabel embraced her, holding onto her for a long moment, and then pressing her lips to Talia's forehead in the gentlest of kisses. A melodic hum filled the air as Isabel's siren power made the air sizzle with energy. A slow heat began at Talia's forehead and trickled down the rest of her body. Something inside her was changing, she could feel it. Her lungs took in air differently, her skin didn't need as much moisture and her throat changed, leaving no ability to sing with siren powers as she once had.

She was now fully human. The call to be in the water had simply faded away. There was a melancholy sorrow about what she'd lost, but she knew that too in time would fade. Isabel leaned back and gazed into Talia's face. Talia stared back at her sister in wonder.

"Thank you, Izzy."

"Enjoy it, little sister." She smiled gently. "Now I must go."

Isabel slipped back into the water and swam away toward the distant pod.

Talia watched the pod for a long moment and then crept down to the master bathroom to examine her face. The bright aquamarine blue of her eyes was gone. They were pale gray once more. She touched her usually dark hair and it now held more hints of gold again. Her skin was less pale and luminescent, but it was warm with an all-too-human hue that she had missed.

"Sweetheart?" Hudson's sleep-roughened voice disturbed the study of her reflection. She turned to see him, bare chested and wearing nothing but pajama pants, standing in the doorway. "I woke to find you gone." He came to Talia, taking her in his arms and hugging her. He did that so often, waking to search for her and embracing her once she was found. He tilted her chin up to gaze into her eyes.

"Isabel came to visit," she said quietly, watching his

face. Would he find her less desirable now the siren in her soul was gone and she was simply human?

"Is she okay?" Hudson, understanding now how deep the bond between Talia and Isabel was, had taken to treating her like a sister whenever they spoke about her. She liked knowing that he was concerned for Isabel.

"Yes, she is. She, um ... gave me a gift." She began to hum softly, purely human vibration escaping her throat, and Hudson's eyes widened, then narrowed slightly. His hands tightened on her shoulders.

"You don't sound like ... wait ... are you...?"

"Human," she replied. "Forever. No more changes."

He stared at her for a long moment, not saying anything and she feared he would want to have the mermaid back.

"Is that okay? You don't miss the siren, do you?" she asked, trying to ignore the anxious knot in her stomach.

"No," he said at once. "You are still my Talia. That's all that matters to me." He leaned down, brushing his mouth over hers before kissing her in a way that made her toes curl. "You're my love, my heart," he whispered. "But is this what you really wanted?"

"Yes. Isabel knew how much I wanted to be human again. Now that I am..."

Hudson grinned. "No more crazy water features in the house then?"

"Probably not," she chuckled. "On the plus side, we

can travel. We might even be able to contact my parents. I don't know what I would say to them, but I want to try. Am I crazy to be this happy?"

"Not at all. We will think of something to say when we find your parents," Hudson promised. "But right now I want to make love to you and pleasure you until I hear my little human scream my name while her legs are wrapped around me when the sun comes up." He scooped her up in his arms, carried her to the master bedroom, and set her down on the bed. She laughed as they tumbled back into the sheets. As she let go of all her worries and kissed the man she loved, she heard the distant song of sirens singing a tale about a stranded little mermaid who had found her way home at last.

Thank you for reading *Stranded*! I plan to write Isabel and Jason's story soon!

To never miss a new release please visit my website below which will give you access to my social media profiles, my newsletter, my private fan group link and my Patreon link where you can get early releases of ebooks, print books, audiobooks, and even special merchandise.

www.laurensmithbooks.com

About the Author

Lauren Smith is an Oklahoma attorney by day, author by night who pens adventurous and edgy romance stories by the light of her smart phone flashlight app. She knew she was destined to be a romance writer when she attempted to re-write the entire *Titanic* movie just to save Jack from drowning. Connecting with readers by writing emotionally moving, realistic and sexy romances no matter what time period is her passion. She's won multiple awards in several romance subgenres including: New England Reader's Choice Awards, Greater Detroit BookSeller's Best Awards, and a Semi-Finalist award for the Mary Wollstonecraft Shelley Award.

To connect with Lauren visit her at:
www.laurensmithbooks.com
lauren@laurensmithbooks.com

facebook.com/LaurenDianaSmith

x.com/LSmithAuthor

instagram.com/laurensmithbooks

bookbub.com/authors/lauren-smith

patreon.com/LSandECBooks

tiktok.com/@laurenandemmabooks

Printed in the USA
CPSIA information can be obtained
at www.ICGtesting.com
JSHW081135090724
66073JS00003B/87